THE WORLD'S
AWESOMEST AIR-BARF

eve Hartley is a sensible man. He has a sensible job, sensible family, lives in a sensible house and drives sensible car. But underneath it all, he longs to be lly. There have been occasional forays into silliness: eve has been a football mascot called Desmond ragon, and has tasted World Record success himself taking part in both a mass yodel and a mass yo-yo. But he wanted more, and so his alter ego – Danny Baker Record Breaker – was created. Steve lives in Lancashire with his wife and teenage daughter.

You can find out more about Steve
on his extremely silly website:
www.stevehartley.net

Also by Steve Hartley

DANNY BAKER RECORD BREAKER
The World's Biggest Bogey

Coming soon

DANNY BAKER RECORD BREAKER
The World's Loudest Armpit Fart

DANNY BAKER RECORD BREAKER
The World's Stickiest Earwax

STEVE HARTLEY

THE WORLD'S
AWESOMEST AIR-BARF

ILLUSTRATED BY KATE PANKHURST

MACMILLAN CHILDREN'S BOOKS

First published 2010 by Macmillan Children's Books
a division of Macmillan Publishers Limited
20 New Wharf Road, London N1 9RR
Basingstoke and Oxford
Associated companies throughout the world
www.panmacmillan.com

ISBN 978-0-330-50917-6

A CIP catalogue record for this book is available from
the British Library.

Printed and bound in the UK by CPI Mackays Chatham ME5 8TD

For Rosie

The Pain
in Spain

WARNING!
THIS STORY
CONTAINS
A GIRL

Sick-bags

To the Keeper of the Records
The Great Big Book of World Records
London

Dear Mr Bibby,

I flew to Spain yesterday and I filled thirteen
sick-bags on the flight. Mum says it was all the
cola and cheese and pickle sandwiches I had at
the airport. She's right, they always make me
barf. That's why I had them!

Is this even close to breaking the record for
filling sick-bags? If it's not, I'll try again on the
way home. I can eat some paella. That
makes me barf even more!

Best wishes
Danny Baker
(Aged nine and a half)

PS We're here because my dad has been
offered a job as the Manager of Real Marisco.
PPS We're staying at the Hotel La Langosta.
It's posh!
PPPS My best friend Matthew has come too, but
I had to count the sick-bags myself. This time,
Matt wouldn't do the maths!

Dear Danny,

Don't even try for this one! You don't stand
a chance, even if you had cheese and pickle
sandwiches *and* paella!

On a non-stop flight between Paris and Sydney,
Marcel Pompidou of Quimper, France, managed
to fill 144 standard-sized airline sick-bags.
Newspapers spread the rumour that Marcel had
four stomachs, like a cow, which was why he was
able to produce so much of the stuff.

The largest number of sick-bags filled on a
single flight is 390, by the 263 contestants
of the Miss Global Warming Beauty Queen
Competition. Halfway through a bumpy flight
to Bongandanga, they had managed to fill every

5

sick-bag on the plane. They were then forced to be sick into their posh hats and handbags.

Officers from *The Great Big Book of World Records* went to Bongandanga to measure this extra sick. It filled another 397 sick-bags, making a total of 787.

Enjoy your visit to Spain.

Best wishes
Eric Bibby
Keeper of the Records

PS Why isn't your dad working for his old club, Walchester United? That would be a dream job, wouldn't it?

Danny and Matthew hurried through the Hotel La Langosta on their way to the beach. They noticed Danny's mum and sister Natalie just ahead of them.

'Hey, Nits,' called Danny. 'Fancy a game of football?'

'As if!' replied Natalie, scornfully. 'We're going shopping.'

'Shopping!' complained Danny. 'That's all girls think about. If this new baby Mum's going to have is a girl, I'm coming to live at your house, Matt.'

They stepped from the cool hotel into the oven-like heat outside.

'Hot,' gasped Danny.

'Cool!' said Matthew.

The two boys headed for the beach, where the Kids' Club at the hotel had arranged a game of football.

It was a great match. The sand was hard and

flat, and many of the kids who were playing were pretty good.

Danny stood in his goalmouth, watching a girl who looked about his age playing for the other team. She was quick, and she did step-overs and back-heels. Matthew was struggling to mark her and, once, the girl even nutmegged him. Danny could see Matt wasn't happy.

She had a shot like a cannon. Several times she blasted a fizzer towards Danny's goal, but Danny was always equal to it.

'You're good,' the girl remarked after Danny had just tipped her diving header around the post.

'You're brilliant!' said Danny.

'I play striker for Bunbury Bantams. I scored thirty-one goals last season,' boasted the girl.

'I *saved* eighty-seven goals *in one game* last season!' replied Danny.

Towards the end of the game, the ball was played low and fast towards the girl. Matthew was close behind her. She went to control the ball, but at the last moment, lifted her foot and let it pass by.

Matthew was completely fooled. The ball sped past him on one side, while the girl slid past him on the other. His legs went in two directions, and he stumbled and landed on his back.

She was through, with only Danny to beat!

Danny moved quickly off his line. The girl glanced up, and shaped to blast a shot. Danny stopped and braced himself to dive, but she didn't shoot. Instead, she chipped the ball high over Danny's head.

He was caught off balance, and had to watch it soar through the clear blue sky and loop down into his empty net.

GOAL!

The girl disappeared in a scrum of kids as her team mobbed her.

Danny knelt on the sand and stared at the ball nestling in the far corner of his goal.

His goal.

Matthew joined him. 'That's the first time anyone's scored past you for –' He thought for a moment.

'*Months!*' Danny blurted out.

'Fourteen months, three weeks, and . . . five days, to be exact.'

Danny and Matthew gazed across the sand as the girl broke away from the throng of kids, did a back somersault, and landed nimbly on her feet.

'Wow!' admired Matthew. 'I can't do that.'

'Neither can I,' admitted Danny. 'I'd better get practising.'

She trotted over to them. She had the reddest hair and greenest eyes Danny had ever seen.

'Hiya.' She grinned. 'I'm Sally Butterworth. See you later in the pool.'

The Girl

Later that afternoon, Danny and Matthew stood in the shallow end of the hotel pool, playing keepy-uppy headers with a beach ball. They had got to twenty-one, when Sally Butterworth launched herself from the edge of the pool and caught the ball in mid-air, before splashing into the water between the two friends.

'Hiya,' spluttered Sally when she surfaced. She was wearing a pair of red goggles and a snorkel. 'Watch this.'

Sally ducked her head beneath the water and blew a towering spout from the snorkel high into the air.

'Wow!' said Danny and Matthew together. It was one of the best super volcanoes they'd ever seen.

'How high did it go?' asked Sally.

'About one and a bit metres,' replied Danny.

'My record's three metres. No one's beat it at my school. Bet you can't beat it either.'

'Bet I can!' said Danny.

He grabbed his own snorkel from the side of the pool, took a deep breath, then dipped beneath the water and blew out as hard as he could. He heard the spluttering, farty sound and knew he hadn't done it right.

'I won!' cheered Sally. 'Want a race? I've got the Bunbury Belugas Swimming Club record for the Fastest Length of Butterfly Ever.'

'Do you like trying to break records then?'

asked Danny with a slight tremble in his voice.

'Yeah. I broke the school squinting record last month. Watch this.'

Sally made her eyes roll to the centre, as though she was looking at something on the end of her nose. Then her right eye drifted across to look away from her. It moved back to the centre, and her left eye slid across to look away. Then *it* returned to the middle once more.

'Ace,' breathed Danny.

'Cool,' agreed Matthew.

'How long did you squint for when you broke the record?' asked Danny.

'Nine hours, sixteen minutes and seven seconds,' answered Sally. 'It would have been longer, but my mum made me stop.'

Matthew hit the beach-ball high in the air. 'Fancy playing a game?'

'Let's play piggy in the middle,' replied Sally. She glanced at Matthew. 'You can be piggy.'

Matthew grumpily took up position in the centre of the shallow end while the other two went to each side. Sally threw the ball high over Matthew's head. He stretched, but couldn't catch it. Danny returned it, but again Matthew was too short.

'Come on,' called Sally after several minutes. 'At this rate you'll break the record for being the piggy in the middle.'

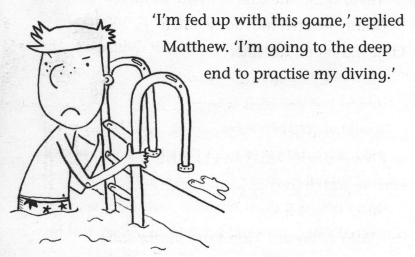

'I'm fed up with this game,' replied Matthew. 'I'm going to the deep end to practise my diving.'

The Prawn

The next morning, Sally Butterworth marched up to Danny and Matthew as they were eating breakfast.

'Hiya, Dan!' she called. 'Hiya, Matt.'

Danny noticed that Sally had a large plaster on her knee.

'How did you do that?' he asked.

'My frisbee got stuck in a tree, so I climbed up to get it. I scraped my knee as I came down. I'm going to have a *massive* scab in a couple of days.'

'Ace,' said Danny.

'Cool . . .' agreed Matthew reluctantly.

Sally leaned over and examined Danny's face.

'Wow! Where did all those freckles come from?' she exclaimed. 'You didn't have those yesterday.'

'I always get zillions of freckles when I've been in the sun.'

'Have you ever counted them? It could be a record,' said Sally.

Danny's mouth fell open in amazement. 'Why didn't *I* think of that?'

'Because you're a boy, and boys don't think of much, my mum says.' Sally continued to stare at Danny's face. 'Would you like me to count them?'

'Counting's *my* job,' insisted Matthew.

Sally began to count anyway. After a while she said, 'You know, Danny, we could try to break the world record for the Longest Kiss.'

Danny glanced anxiously at Matthew. 'Matt, I think you *had* better do the freckle counting.'

Matthew grabbed Danny and pulled him away. 'We've got to go,' he told Sally.

'See you later, Dan,' she called as the boys raced away.

'Kissing!' said Matthew. 'Gross!'

'Yeah,' agreed Danny. 'Girl-germs! Mega-gross!'

'Lucky I was there to rescue you. *I'll* count your freckles later.'

'Thanks, Matt. I'll have more by tonight anyway.'

Just after lunch, Danny and Matthew arrived at El Estadio del Mar, Real Marisco's home ground, with Danny's mum, dad and sister, Natalie. A large crowd of fans, all wearing the pale pink shirts of Real Marisco, were waiting to greet their possible new manager and his family. They began to cheer loudly, and a flamenco band struck up a jaunty tune, playing with gusto so they could be heard above the din.

The family smiled and waved to the crowd. An odd movement caught Danny's eye. He glanced to his left and was horrified to see a six-foot-tall pink sea creature running towards him. The monster's two long antennae and four of its six outstretched pink legs waggled threateningly.

Before Danny could move or cry out, the creature grabbed him in a fierce, rubbery clinch, and lifted him off the ground. Danny stared into one of its shiny black eyes.

'Matt –' gasped Danny. 'Help!'

Matthew grasped the beast by its feathery, fan-shaped tail.

'Let go of my mate!' he yelled, swinging the creature round.

Cameras flashed. The band played on. The crowd cheered even louder. There was a tearing sound, and without warning, the monster's tail came off in Matthew's hands.

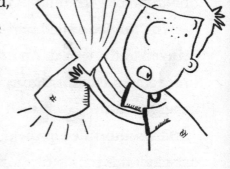

'Arrrrgh!' screamed the sea creature. 'Mi cola!'

It let go of Danny and turned to face Matthew. In the hole where the tail had been, Danny saw a bottom wearing a pair of tight purple underpants.

The tailless monster
held two pink claws
over its rear end and
scuttled away through
the crowd.

Mum laughed.
'I wish the video
camera wasn't broken,'
she said. 'I'd have loved to get that on film!'

'Thanks, Matt,' said Danny. 'What was *that*?'

Danny's dad was red-faced with laughter.

'Didn't I tell you?' he replied. 'Real Marisco
are known as "Las Gambas", which means "The
Prawns" in Spanish. That was their mascot, Gogo
La Gamba.'

Matthew gazed at the giant pink tail he still held
in his hands.

'Their mascot's a prawn?' he asked
disbelievingly.

'That's even worse than Wally
the Wall!' exclaimed Danny.

(Wally the Wall was Walchester

United's mascot. He was a brick wall, with legs.)

A man walked towards them, laughing heartily. He shook Dad's hand and then kissed Danny's mum on both cheeks.

Dad turned to the children and introduced the man.

'Kids, this is Señor Pez, the Director of Real Marisco.' He leaned over to the boys and whispered, 'He's the Boss.'

'Delighted to meet you!' said Señor Pez, shaking Danny's hand.

He turned to greet Matthew, who was still clutching the prawn's giant tail.

'I'm sorry,' mumbled Matthew. 'It just came off in my hand.' Señor Pez laughed again. 'Do not be upset, young señor. I hate that stupid prawn.'

He took the tail from Matthew and put it under his arm. Then he kissed Danny's sister Natalie on the cheek. She blushed a deeper pink than the giant prawn.

'Señor Baker, Señora Baker, in two weeks' time, it is Marisco's annual Festival of Deliverance. In honour of your visit, the town council of Marisco would like your son Danny to be "El Periquito".'

'Who's El Periquito?' asked Danny.

'A . . . how do you say it in English? A butterygar?'

Danny frowned. 'A butterygar?'

Matthew flicked quickly through his English-Spanish dictionary. '"Periquito" means budgerigar,' he whispered to Danny.

Señor Pez smiled, and held his hands as though praying. 'The butterygar was sent from heaven to save our town from disaster, many, many years ago,' he explained.

'What do I have to do?'

'Dress up as a bird, climb a tall tree, whistle a special tune and collect caterpillars in a bucket.'

'Ace!' yelled Danny.

'Cool!' agreed Matthew.

Freckles and Jenny-ticks

Hotel La Langosta
Marisco
Spain

Dear Mr Bibby,

It's me again, Danny. The Hotel La Langosta is Ace. I've met a girl called Sally Butterworth, who is brilliant at football and likes breaking records! She's got double-jointed elbows and she can climb trees and wiggle her ears and squint. What's the world record for squinting?

It's really sunny here, and I've got 1,246 freckles on

1,2+6 freckles

my face. It would have been more, but my mum spotted them, and got me with factor 5 million suncream.

factor
5 MILLION
SUN CREAM

Matt counted my freckles using a magic marker pen to mark each one, so he didn't count any twice. The trouble is, the ink won't wash off, so now I've got 1,246 blue dots on my face as well as the freckles.

I think it looks Ace.

Matthew thinks it looks cool.

My sister Natalie thinks it looks stupid.

Sally Butterworth thinks it looks like warpaint.

My mum thinks it looks like a disease.

My dad thinks that if he joins up all the dots, he could make a picture of England's winning goal in the 1966 World Cup Final.

Have I broken the freckles record?

Best wishes
Danny Baker

PS While I'm here in Marisco, I have to dress up
as a budgie called El Periquito, climb
a tall tree, whistle a special tune
and catch caterpillars in a bucket.
I'm not sure why, but I'm going to
have a go! I'll see if I can whistle for
longer and catch more caterpillars than anyone
else has ever done.

El Periquito.

ARE YOU A RECORD
BREAKER ?

Dear Danny,

Thanks for your letter. Sally Butterworth
sounds an interesting girl.

Your attempt to break the world record for
Freckles on a Single Face was superb, and was
only 453 freckles short. Another day or two
might have given you the extra needed. But
don't be cross with your mum - she was doing
the right thing using suncream on you. Better
safe than sorry!

You asked about the world record for squinting.
That is held by Vinay Adatia, of Mysore, in
India. Unfortunately, Vinay wasn't *trying* to
break the record. When he was ten years old, a
mosquito landed on the end of his nose. Young

Vinay screwed up his face, and squinted to look at it. At that very moment, the wind changed direction, and Vinay got stuck like that.

He stayed stuck like that for the next fifteen years, four months and nineteen days.

Of course, the wind changed again many, many times during those years, but Vinay's squint was so well and truly jammed, it wouldn't budge.

Eventually, Vinay got a job looking after Radha, the sacred elephant, at the Hindu shrine near Dooda Bellalu. One morning, he was washing Radha's hind parts with a scrubbing brush, when the elephant broke wind so hard and with such a horrible pong, that not only did it blow Vinay's hat off, it blew his squint off too! He is now a famous Bollywood film star.

The record for Non Wind-assisted Squinting is

five days, sixteen hours and thirty-one minutes,
held by Franz Überburger, of Wörgl, Austria.
His attempt came to an end when he fell asleep
from exhaustion, and his eyes returned to their
normal position.

If you are going to attempt the squinting
record, Danny, be like Franz Überburger, and
make sure you try it out of the wind, and
away from sacred elephants. Getting stuck
with a squint would definitely affect your
goalkeeping!

Best wishes
Eric Bibby
Keeper of the Records

Danny and Sally sat on the low wall that enclosed the garden of the Hotel La Langosta. Nearby, Matthew played table tennis with Natalie.

Click-clock, click-clock, click-clock.

Sally stuck her tongue out at Danny. It rolled into a perfect tube.

'Now you try,' she said.

Danny tried, but failed. His tongue just twisted, or bent inwards. 'I can't do it,' he moaned.

Sally shrugged. 'My mum says it's jenny-ticks.'

'What's jenny-ticks?'

'I don't know – something in your body that decides if your tongue can roll into a tube or not.'

Sally demonstrated again and then said, 'Let's try to break that record for the Longest Kiss.'

'No, I don't think so,' answered Danny.

Click-clock, click-clock, click-clock.

'Why not?' Sally leaned her face closer to Danny's.

Danny gulped.

Her face was so close, it filled his view. Everything had gone silent, and all Danny could hear was his heart bashing inside his chest. Suddenly, Sally's face disappeared, and a ping-pong bat filled his view instead.

'Fancy a game, you two?' asked Matthew.

'What?' Danny blinked, and gazed up at Matthew.

'You and me against Nat the Nit and Sally Butterfingers.' Sally glared at Matthew as he yanked Danny off the chair and dragged him over to the ping-pong table.

Natalie grinned at her brother and sang, 'Danny's kissed his girlfriend, Danny's kissed his girlfriend.'

'I didn't!' protested Danny.

'Well, you would have, if Matt hadn't stepped in.'

Danny blushed prawn-pink.

'No I wouldn't,' he said quietly. 'And she's not my girlfriend. Come on, let's play.'

Click-clock, click-clock, click-clock.

Every time Danny glanced across the table at Sally, she smiled at him.

Matthew smacked Danny on the top of his arm with his ping-pong bat. 'Keep your mind on the game!' he hissed. 'They're winning!'

Danny tried. He tried hard, but it seemed that every time he hit the ball, it either pinged into the net, or ponged on to the floor. Finally he looped a weak shot into the air to make sure it got over the net. Natalie pounced on it, and smashed the ball back at him.

'Yessssssss! The Girls beat the Boys!'

Natalie and Sally high-fived, and did a silly victory dance around the table.

'See you at dinner, losers!' yelled Natalie as she walked away laughing.

Matthew glared at Danny.

'You were useless,' he snarled.

'You . . . you kept getting in my way,' countered Danny.

'*Me?* You couldn't get the ball on the table!'

'Yeah, because –'

Before Danny could finish, Matthew threw his bat down on the table and stormed off.

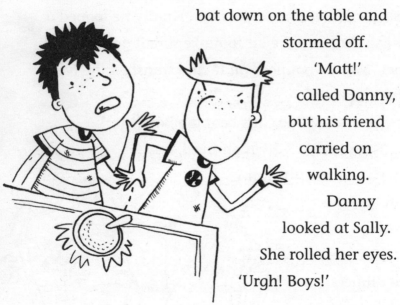

'Matt!' called Danny, but his friend carried on walking.

Danny looked at Sally. She rolled her eyes. 'Urgh! Boys!'

Silly Sausage

Hotel La Langosta
Marisco
Spain

Dear Mr Bibby

I'm the Marisco Junior Chorizo-pushing
Champion! This morning some of the Kids'
Club here at the hotel entered the annual
championships. You have to use your nose to push
a Spanish sausage along the ground for as far
as you can. It was fun!

Matthew dropped out pretty quickly, and so did
all the other Kids, except for Sally Butterworth.
My Knees and hands and back were Killing me,
but I wouldn't give up and neither would
Sally. In the end, Sally had to stop when
the big scab came off her Knee, but I

Sally's
Knee

went on for another fifteen laps of the course.
I pushed the chorizo sausage for 8.88 km.

Matthew says that Sally let me win, but I think
he's just jealous.

I won a gold medal shaped like a sausage.
It's not *real* gold, but it's still Ace. The local
chorizo-pushing team have asked me if I want
to be in their squad when we come out to
live here. They've never won the Spanish
Chorizo-pushing Cup, and want to get the
best players they can. I might do it!

medal

Can you tell me, has anyone ever
pushed a chorizo further than 8.88 km? I'm very
stiff and sore today, and I've got to do the 'El
Periquito' thing in a few days. I hope I've not
spoilt my chances to break *that* record.

Best wishes
Danny

ARE YOU A RECORD
BREAKER ?

Dear Danny

Congratulations on winning the Marisco Junior
Chorizo-pushing Championship. I'm sorry, but
your excellent performance was many shoves
short of the world record.

In 2000, to celebrate the birth of the new
millennium, Luis 'La Nariz' Lopo set off from
Madrid in an attempt to push a chorizo sausage
around the world with his nose, in a symbolic
gesture to bring about world peace. He had
pushed the sausage for 3,932.6 km, when his
route took him across Red Square in Moscow,
Russia, during a military parade. Tragically,
because 'La Nariz' was so close to the ground,
he wasn't seen, and was run over by a Russian
T-90S tank.

Amazingly, although the tank squashed most
of Luis, it completely missed his nose *and* the
chorizo, both of which can now be seen, stuffed
and on display, in the museum of his home town,
Fisgón.

Good luck with the 'El Periquito' ceremony,
Danny.

Best wishes
Eric Bibby
Keeper of the Records

It was early in the morning on the day of
the ceremony. Sally Butterworth
sat close to Danny, trying to
teach him how to waggle
his ears. Danny's face
twitched and convulsed
with the effort.

Sally grabbed
Danny's ears, and
wiggled them.

'You need to move
this part of your head –'
she slapped him on the forehead – 'not *that* part of
your head.'

'It's no good,' complained Danny. 'I can't do it.'

Sally smiled.

Oh-oh! thought Danny. She's got that 'Kiss-Me-
Quick' look again!

He felt someone grab his arm and drag him on
to his feet. It was Matthew.

'Come on, it's time you put your budgie costume
on,' said his friend.

Danny yanked his arm free of Matthew's grasp.

'Stop dragging me around, and telling me what to do,' he snapped.

'I'm just looking out for you,' replied Matthew.

'I can look out for myself, *thanks*. You're worse than Mum.'

'Yeah?'

'Yeah.'

'Right, if that's how you feel, you stay here, canoodling with your *girlfriend*.'

Sally giggled.

'I will if I want to,' said Danny. 'You're just jealous.'

'Yeah, right!'

'Yeah, *right!*'

Matthew strode away.

'I hope the caterpillars get you, Budgie-face!' he called over his shoulder.

Danny tried to think of something snotty to say back to Matthew. He couldn't. They had never fallen out before.

'Get lost!' he shouted, but he didn't really mean it.

Sally rolled her eyes again. 'Urgh! Boys!'

El Periquito

In the hotel bedroom, Danny's mum put down the
video camera that she had been trying to mend in
time for the ceremony. Then she helped him put on
the bird costume.

'You're very quiet,' she said as Danny stepped
into his pink, three-toed budgie feet. 'Is everything
all right?'

Danny shrugged. 'Yeah.'

Mum began to pull the bright blue
stretchy tights up Danny's legs.

'Mum, why am I doing this?' he
grumbled.

'I thought you wanted to do
it.'

Danny sighed. 'I do, but
what's it all about?'

Mum held up the budgie
suit. It was covered in vivid
sky-blue feathers, with black

and white striped wings sown along the arms, and a short, pointed black and white tail.

'There's an ancient tree in the centre of the town square that is supposed to have been planted by Saint Peter of the Fishes, Marisco's patron saint. The locals believe that while the tree is alive their fishermen will continue to catch plenty of seafood . . .'

Danny put his arms into the budgie wings. Mum joined the two parts of the body together, and began to fumble with the zip.

'Over a hundred years ago, the tree was infested with a plague of caterpillars that all hatched out on the same night and began to munch away at the leaves. The townsfolk prayed for a miracle to save their tree, and the miracle arrived the next morning, when a blue and white budgie flew into town and ate all the caterpillars.'

She pulled the zip carefully towards Danny's neck.

'El Periquito – the budgie – saved the tree from certain death and saved the fishermen from going out of business. As it munched away, the bird filled the square with its chirpy song. Then, when it had eaten every caterpillar, the budgie flew away, never to return.'

Mum slid the tight white hood over Danny's head and fitted it snugly around his chin. She smoothed down the four black feathered spots around his neck and fixed the stubby yellow beak over his nose.

'The caterpillars still hatch out on the same day every year, but there's usually only a few hundred or so. A young boy climbs the tree dressed as El Periquito, collects them in a bucket and whistles the "Budgie Song", which I'm told was composed in 1876 by a man named Manuel de Compostela.'

She straightened the suit around Danny's body, and smiled.

'Lovely. Go and look at yourself.'

Danny rustled over to the full-length mirror on the wardrobe door. He lifted his arms to spread his wings, and whistled a few bars of the Budgie Song.

'Ace,' he said.

But he didn't really mean it.

Half an hour later, Danny stood in the town square of Marisco, dressed in the budgie suit and carrying a bucket. The sun had risen above the roofs of the old pink buildings that formed the square, and Danny was already hot.

It seemed like the whole town had come out to see him. The same band that had greeted them at the stadium played the same loud, cheerful tune. Gogo La Gamba, the giant prawn mascot of Real Marisco, had a new tail and was there to cheer Danny on.

Danny's dad stood next to him. He glanced around the crowd.

'Why did Matt decide to stay at the hotel?' he asked.

Danny shrugged. 'Don't know.'

'Have you two fallen out?'

Danny shrugged again, but said nothing. He wished he hadn't told Matthew to 'Get lost!'

Sally Butterworth was standing nearby and blew him a kiss. Danny rolled his eyes.

The Mayoress of Marisco, Señora Juanita Delgardo, held up her hand, and the band and the crowd fell silent.

'Today is the anniversary of our Deliverance from the Plague of Caterpillars,' she announced. 'It is the day the caterpillars hatch out in our sacred tree, and the day El Periquito climbs into the tree to collect them.'

The crowd applauded.

'I now ask Father Ignatius, from the Church of the Holy Budgerigar, to bless El Periquito and send him on his sacred task.'

An old priest stepped forward, placing his hand on Danny's head. The priest mumbled a

prayer in Latin and sprinkled Danny with Holy water. He crossed himself, then gestured for Danny to climb the tree.

Danny marched forward to the ladders propped up against the trunk of the massive old tree. A net stretched around the base of the tree to catch him if he fell.

'When do I start to whistle?' he asked.

'From the moment you pick up the first caterpillar to the moment you collect the final one,' answered Father Ignatius. 'El Periquito sang as he munched, from start to finish.'

Danny had been learning the Budgie Song for days. He pursed his lips, and blew. The notes trilled and echoed around the silent square. When he got to the top of the ladder and climbed into the tree, the crowd cheered.

Danny waved. He scanned
the crowd quickly, to see if
Matthew had turned up
to watch him after all,
but he couldn't see his
friend anywhere. Sally
waved back at him.

Danny turned and looked at the branches
around him. He gasped.

'What is wrong, Señor Danny? Are there no
caterpillars?' called the Mayoress.

'There are *thousands* of them!'

The Mayoress went pale and held on to the
priest's arm.

'*Thousands?*'

'Millions!' confirmed Danny.
'They're everywhere!'

He stared goggle-eyed
at the green and yellow
caterpillars that were
crawling over every inch
of bark and leaf.

The band fell silent. Hushed, horrified whispers rippled through the townsfolk.

'It has happened again!' said Father Ignatius. 'The plague has returned!'

'Shall we send more people up into the tree?' suggested the Mayoress.

'No!' cried Father Ignatius. 'It must be El Periquito who collects the caterpillars!'

The old priest gazed up at Danny with red, watery eyes.

'Only Danny Baker can save us now!'

The Kissing Tree

Danny toiled all day in the scorching sun, working his way higher and higher into the tree, picking the small wriggling creatures from underneath leaves, knocking them off twigs and dropping them into buckets. All the time he worked, Danny whistled the Budgie Song.

His limbs ached, his lips ached, but he carried on collecting and he carried on whistling, only stopping to drink water.

The sun dropped lower in the sky. The light began to fade. The mood of the people gathered around the tree was sombre and tense. They all stood gazing up anxiously at Danny as he crawled to the tip of the final branch.

He dropped the last caterpillar into his bucket.

'Finished!' he called hoarsely, and carried on whistling.

The roar from the throng of people watching Danny echoed around the square. It was as though Real Marisco had won the Cup!

Father Ignatius put his hands together and offered a silent prayer of thanks.

Danny began to pick his way slowly and painfully back down through the branches, but then stopped. His limbs and lips, tight and tense all day from climbing, gripping and whistling, had finally given up. Danny's body and mouth locked tight with cramp.

He couldn't move a muscle.

He couldn't say a word.

He was stuck.

He heard someone below shout, 'Help him!'

Then he heard Sally Butterworth yell, 'I'll save you, Danny!'

Sally raced from the crowd and scurried up the ladder. In seconds she had clambered into the tree and reached the branch where Danny was perched. She smiled at him.

'Your lips are stuck in *kissing* position,' she said.

No! thought Danny. Help!

But there was no one to help. Sally leaned forward and planted her lips firmly on Danny's.

'Awwwwww,' cooed the crowd.

Urrrrrrgh! thought Danny.

He looked past Sally into the crowded square and spotted his sister Natalie laughing at him. Even worse, his mum had finally fixed the video camera and was *filming* the kiss.

He could hear Natalie singing, 'Danny and Sally, sitting in a tree, K-I-S-S-I-N-G.'

The kiss went on . . .

Urrrrrrrrrgh!

and on . . .

Urrrrrrrrrrrgh!

and on . . .

Urrrrrrrrrrrrrgh!

and on . . .

Urrrrrrrrrrrrrrgh!

Danny sent up his own silent prayer. *Help!*

And his prayer was answered.

He heard leaves rustling and a branch creaking, and there was Matthew, beside them in the tree.

'Now that's enough of *that*!' ordered Matthew. He tried to drag Sally away, but she clung on tight.

'Sally,' he shouted. 'There's a *massive* spider on your back!'

Danny saw Sally's eyes widen in horror. She pulled away quickly.

'Arrrrrrrrrgh!' she screamed. 'Get it off! Get it off!'

Matthew pretended to brush something off her.

He blew out his cheeks and shook his head. 'Wow,

that was *huge*,' he gasped. He wiggled his fingers. 'It had *really* hairy legs! There must be loads more of them around here.'

Sally screamed. In seconds she was out of the tree and standing in the square next to her mother.

Matthew grinned. 'I think Silly Butterworm has just broken the world record for the Fastest Climbing Out of a Tree to Escape an Invisible Spider, don't you?'

Danny looked at Matthew and raised his eyebrows, which was the only part of him he could move. Thanks, Matt, he thought. You saved me.

'I'm sorry, Dan,' said Matthew.

Danny twitched his eyebrows once. So am I, Matt, he thought.

Matthew understood and nodded. 'We will never, *ever* fall out, *ever* again.'

Danny raised his eyebrows twice: No.

'Do you see what happens when I'm not around to look out for you?'

Danny twitched his eyebrows once: Yeah.

The two boys perched side by side in the tree, and

looked down on the people celebrating in the town square. After a while, Matthew sighed.

'Have you realized that when your dad gets the job as manager of Real Marisco, you'll have to live here and I'll have to go back to England?' he said.

Danny frowned: What?

Matthew stared at Danny sadly.

'We'll probably never see each other again,' he said quietly. 'Ever.'

Danny's eyebrows nearly twitched off his face: Noooooooooooooo!

Danny Baker - Record Breaker

Hotel La Langosta
Marisco
Spain

Dear Mr Bibby,

I dressed up as El Periquito and collected 14,975 caterpillars. I didn't know it at
the time, but as I passed
the buckets down to
Father Ignatius, Matthew
was counting the caterpillars
in each one, so that I could write
to you with my score. I also stayed in the
tree whistling for ten hours and twenty-three
minutes. When I'd finished, I had cramp in my
whole body. I couldn't move for fifty-three

hours and sixteen minutes. Surely one of these
must be a record?

Best wishes
Danny

ARE YOU A RECORD
BREAKER?

Dear Danny

Fantastic! You saved Marisco from disaster,
and claimed not just one, but *two* El
Periquito world records. You beat the previous
caterpillar-collecting record by more than
thirteen thousand, and whistled in the tree
for nearly ten hours longer than anyone had
ever done before. I'm sure your records will
remain for a very long time, possibly for ever.
Congratulations!

Unfortunately, however, the long attack of
cramp you suffered is not a record.

In 1966, Harriet Snood of Tolpuddle attempted to
break the world record for dancing 'The Twist'.
After sixty-nine hours and seventeen minutes,

her whole body locked like stone.
Doctors have been unable to thaw out
Harriet's frozen muscles even
to this day. She is still stuck
in twisting position! With
every minute that passes, she
adds to her record, which as I
write is 15,696 days, 3 hours
and 6 minutes. Harriet now has
a successful career as a 'Living Sculpture'.

Finally, Danny, you didn't tell me about the
kiss!

Your mum sent me the video she made of you
and Sally Butterworth kissing in the tree. I'm
delighted to tell you that you and Sally have
set a new world record, and I have included
two extra certificates, one for you and one for
Sally. Would you please pass it on to her?

Congratulations on breaking three world

records at once, Danny!

Best wishes

Eric Bibby

Keeper of the Records

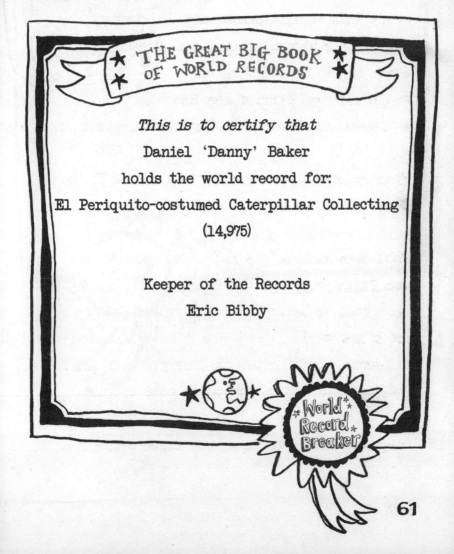

THE GREAT BIG BOOK OF WORLD RECORDS

This is to certify that
Daniel 'Danny' Baker
holds the world record for:
El Periquito-costumed Caterpillar Collecting
(14,975)

Keeper of the Records
Eric Bibby

World Record Breaker

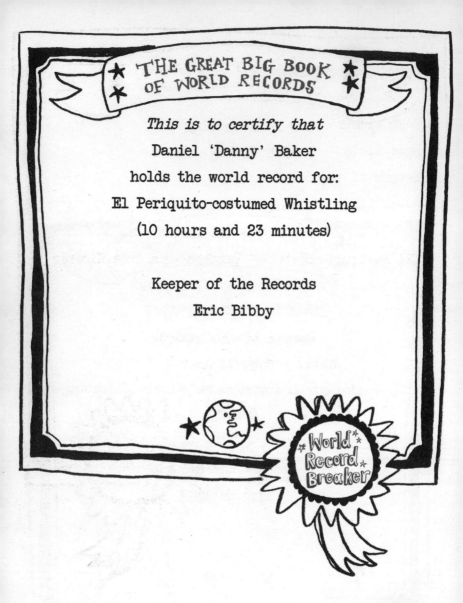

THE GREAT BIG BOOK OF WORLD RECORDS

This is to certify that
Daniel 'Danny' Baker
holds the world record for:
El Periquito-costumed Whistling
(10 hours and 23 minutes)

Keeper of the Records
Eric Bibby

World Record Breaker

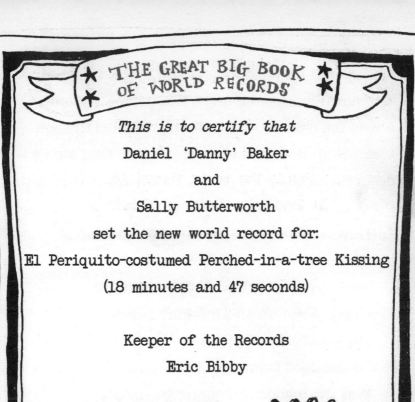

THE GREAT BIG BOOK OF WORLD RECORDS

This is to certify that
Daniel 'Danny' Baker
and
Sally Butterworth
set the new world record for:
El Periquito-costumed Perched-in-a-tree Kissing
(18 minutes and 47 seconds)

Keeper of the Records
Eric Bibby

World Record Breaker

Danny and his dad kicked a ball around the beach. The sun shimmered orange, like a huge satsuma, above the calm blue sea. Danny dribbled the ball towards his dad, and nutmegged him. Dad toppled on to the sand with a groan. Danny came over and sat down next to him.

'Have you and Matthew made friends again?' asked Dad.

'Yeah, 'course we have,' replied Danny.

'Good. What about Sally Butterworth?'

'She's going home today.'

Dad nudged Danny with his elbow and winked.

'Was she a good girlfriend?' he asked.

Danny blushed prawn-pink, and looked away.

'She was a good *footballer*,' he answered.

Dad laughed and ruffled Danny's hair. He nodded at the view. 'Fantastic, isn't it?'

'Yeah.'

'Do you like it here in Marisco?'

'Yeah, it's Ace.'

'Would you like to live here for good?'

Danny pushed his feet into the sand and hugged

his knees. 'Could Matt come and live here too?'

'No, of course not. His mum and dad couldn't just pack up and move out here because we have.'

Dad put his arm around Danny's shoulders.

'Honestly, where would you rather live, here or in England?'

Danny took a deep breath. 'In England!' he blurted out. 'I'm sorry, Dad. I'd be OK living here, honest, but I'd have to spend every day wearing factor 5 million suncream, and I'd miss the rain at home, and I'd miss my school football team, and . . . I'd miss Matt. He's my best mate.'

Dad frowned and looked thoughtful. 'Yeah, I thought you'd say that.' A grin spread slowly across his face. 'Good thing I turned down the Manager's job here at Real Marisco then.'

'What?'

'Walchester United want me to be their goalkeeping coach. It's my Dream Job, Danny. I start as soon as we get back.'

Danny jumped up. 'Are you serious?'

'Totally.'

Danny punched the air, put his head back and yelled, 'IN . . . THE . . . NET!'

When they got back to the hotel, Sally Butterworth was waiting in reception for the bus to go back to the airport. Matthew was there too, to make sure she didn't miss it.

'Bye, Danny,' said Sally as the bus pulled up.

'Er . . . bye, Sally.' Danny stood well back, in case she had any goodbye kissing in mind.

'Did you know, Father Ignatius, of the Church of the Holy Budgerigar, has said that from now on "El Periquito" must be kissed by a beautiful young girl before he comes down from the tree? Why don't we come back next year and try to break our own record?'

Danny and Matthew looked at each other.

'*Not* Ace!' cried Danny.

'*Not* cool!' agreed Matthew.

Sally got on board the bus and waved sadly through the back window as it pulled away.

Danny's mum walked up to them.

'Have you two boys packed yet?' she asked. 'We'll be leaving after lunch.'

Danny grinned at Matthew. 'Come on, Matt – cola and paella for lunch,' he said. 'I've got sick-bags to fill!'

The Super-Secret Ingredient

WARNING!
LOW-FLYING
COWPATS
AHEAD

The Pongy Potion

Crag Top Farm, Puddlethorpe

Dear Mr Bibby

I'm staying on Grandma Florrie and Grandad Nobby's farm. It's slippy and slimy and whiffs for England! My best friend Matthew's here too. We're having fun tidying up cowpats, making mudslides, eating beans, feeding the pigs with something called Swill, and brewing up a Pongy Potion in a bucket! This morning I stacked five dried cowpats on my head and walked 6.7 km. I would have gone further, but it started to rain and the cowpats turned to mush and dribbled down all over me. My grandma says 'A bit of muck never hurt anyone.' I don't think my mum would say that. Did I break a record?

Best wishes
Danny Baker

cowpat

mushy cowpat

To Mr E. Bibby

The Keeper of the Records

The Great Big Book of World Records

London

A&E YOU A RECORD BREAKER ?

Dear Danny

Thank you for your postcard. I had no idea
that the Painless Pig-tail Curler was invented
in Puddlethorpe.

I *know* you and Matthew will have lots of fun
on your grandparents' farm, but I wouldn't
try any cowpat records if I were you. There are
Professional Cowpatters all over the world who
compete in tournaments, either individually
or in teams, battling to be the best at cowpat
balancing, cowpat rolling, cowpat tossing,
cowpat spinning and cowpat polo. Tournament-
standard cowpats are produced from carefully
bred Culworth Curly-horn cows, which are fed
a special diet to give the pats a regular
consistency. They are baked in clay ovens for

one hour and thirteen minutes exactly, at a temperature of 190^{0} centigrade (Gas Mark 5), and then cut to the regulation 35 cm-diameter size. All record attempts are strictly controlled by the WPCA (World Professional Cowpatting Association).

However, don't let that stop you having fun with cowpats!

Best wishes
Eric Bibby
Keeper of the Records

PS Is your grandad the same Norbert 'Nobby' Baker who broke the world record for Blindfold One-foot Keepy-uppies in 1968?

Danny and Matthew sat at the big kitchen table, eating lunch. On the plates in front of them, Grandma Florrie's home-made baked beans  dripped and dribbled over the toast. Grandma was proud of her beans, and gave them to the boys at every meal whether they wanted them or not. 'They'll put hairs on your chest,' she told them. Every night, they stood in front of the bathroom mirror and checked, but so far nothing had happened.

Grandma sat in a battered old armchair in her bright floral apron and green wellington boots, and got on with her knitting. She was making pink bootees for Mum's new baby.

Danny frowned. 'How do you know the baby's going to be a girl?' he asked.

'I can feel it in my waters,' she replied mysteriously.

Grandad Nobby sat at the table with the boys, reading Mr Bibby's letter. The grubby old flat cap that he always wore was pushed back on his head. Danny couldn't remember seeing Grandad without his cap – he suspected he even slept in it.

'Aye, Danny, that's me,' confirmed Grandad Nobby. 'You're not the only one in the family who likes to break records, you know.'

'It must be jenny-ticks,' commented Matthew.

Grandad walked over to a cupboard and rummaged around inside.

Danny and Matthew took their chance while Grandma and Grandad weren't looking, and quickly scraped most of their beans into a bowl they had hidden under the table.

'Ah, here it is,' muttered Grandad after a few seconds, and handed Danny a picture frame.

Beneath the glass, he saw a familiar-looking certificate.

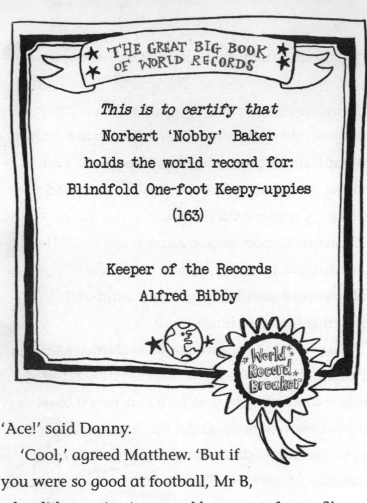

THE GREAT BIG BOOK OF WORLD RECORDS

This is to certify that
Norbert 'Nobby' Baker
holds the world record for:
Blindfold One-foot Keepy-uppies
(163)

Keeper of the Records
Alfred Bibby

World Record Breaker

'Ace!' said Danny.

'Cool,' agreed Matthew. 'But if
you were so good at football, Mr B,
why did you give it up and become a farmer?'

'Tell Matt your story, Grandad,' urged Danny.
'Tell him about the Rotting Chowhabunga.'

Grandad's brow furrowed as though he was
remembering something painful. 'I didn't *want* to

give up football, Matt,' he said. 'I was *forced* to give it up.'

'Why?'

'Injury,' he replied, and held his left knee.

'Was it a bad tackle?' guessed Matthew. 'Did another player go over the top of the ball? Did you land badly going for a header?'

Grandad Nobby was silent for a moment. He shook his head slowly.

'I trod on a seed-pod,' he said eventually.

Matthew stared at him blankly.

'I was on a tour of Brazil with Walchester United. I'd heard that the Rotting Chowhabunga plant was about to flower in the jungle. It's supposed to have the Stinkiest Flower in the world, and local people say that anyone who gets too close to its horrible stench is instantly turned to stone!'

Matthew's jaw dropped. 'Is that true?'

'Of course not!' chuckled Grandad. 'It's just a myth! People can't be petrified by a pong!' He ruffled Matthew's hair. 'Anyway, the Rotting Chowhabunga only blooms in the wild and the petals last for just one day, so I hurried out into the jungle to see it. But when I got to the spot, I was too late: the flower had died. As I turned away, I slipped on a seed-pod that had fallen on the ground, and twisted my knee so badly I never played football again.'

He rubbed his leg once more.

'A seed from the pod got stuck in my sock. I found it when I got home a week later, so I planted the seed in some soil and it grew. Ever since, I've been determined to be the first person to get the Rotting Chowhabunga to bloom in a pot. That plant ended my football career, and I'm not going to let it beat me again!'

Matthew glanced nervously around the room. 'Where is it?'

'It's in a pot, out near the vegetable patch,' answered Grandma. 'If your Grandad ever wins the battle, and it's even *half* as stinky as he says it'll be, then I don't want that thing anywhere near my house.'

'How long have you been trying to make it

flower?' asked Matthew.

'Thirty-nine years,' replied Grandad. 'I use soil from my compost heap, and feed it with the gunge from my barrel of liquid cowpats. The plant grows beautifully, but I can't find that one special ingredient that will make it flower.' He shook his head thoughtfully. 'I will one day though, you see if I don't.'

Suddenly, Danny had an idea. He glanced over at Matthew and winked.

Grandad sighed. 'I don't have much luck with my veggies either. It's the Puddlethorpe Annual Country Fair in a few days, and I never win first prize. Every year, Ernie Slack manages to beat me into second place. I don't know how he does it.'

After lunch, Danny and Matthew carried a bucket of swill across the farmyard to feed Fish, Chips and Peas, Grandma's three little pigs. Then they went to check on the Pongy Potion, which was brewing in a big metal bucket behind the pigsty. Its contents were cooking slowly in the sun, and for days the boys had been adding all sorts of ingredients to it.

'I've been thinking,' said Danny. 'Do you reckon our Pongy Potion could be the special ingredient Grandad needs to make his Rotting Chowhabunga flower? Let's add it to the gunge in his cowpat barrel and see what happens.'

'I don't *want* it to flower, if it'll turn us into stone,' remarked Matthew.

'Don't be daft, Matt! You heard Grandad – it's just a myth!'

Matthew frowned, but said nothing more.

'Urgh!' cried Danny, covering his face with his arm as they approached the bucket. 'It's getting *really* pongy!'

He held his nose, took off the lid, and the boys peeked inside. It looked like a giant had been sick in the bucket. It was filled almost to the brim with a thick, lumpy greeny-yellowy soup. Wisps of green steam drifted slowly upwards from the surface.

Matthew reached into the pocket of his jeans, and unfolded a piece of paper:

Pongy Potion Recipe

3 milk bottlefuls of muddy puddle water

99 tea bags (used and soggy)

1 dollop of mud

5 squirts of washing-up liquid

A splodge of cold mashed potato

3 apple cores (Granny Smith's)

A brushful of grey hair (Granny Baker's)

Granny's hair

77 carrot tops

1 pineapple yogurt with bits in

A sprinkle of crunched-up eggshells

2 banana skins (squished)

4 rotten tomatoes (squashed)

stinky

2 balls of donkey doo-doo

3 handfuls of mouldy straw

A sweaty sock with a hole in the big toe

Half a can of lemonade with the fizz all

gone

ear-wax

4 finger-scoops of earwax

A munched-up Garibaldi biscuit

A teaspoonful of toenail clippings (assorted)

'I don't remember putting that mushroom in there,' said Danny, tipping in the beans they had saved from lunch.

'We didn't. That's grown since yesterday,' replied Matthew. He wrote '1 mushroom' and '1 bowl of Grandma's home-made baked beans' at the bottom of his list.

The Pongy Potion hissed angrily and a small bubble of gas popped on to the surface. Danny plunged a rusty old trowel into the concoction, and turned it over a few times. The Pongy Potion

gurgled and more bubbles burst from the brew. The smell smashed into Danny's face, drilled up his nostrils and exploded through his brain. He reeled backwards, coughing and gasping for breath.

'Quick!' he spluttered. 'Put the lid back on, before it gets out!'

Matthew slammed the lid on to the bucket and they scuttled away to safety.

'Mega-ace!' cried Danny.

'Mega-cool!' agreed Matthew.

A Wiggle of Worms

Crag Top Farm
Puddlethorpe

Dear Mr Bibby

Today I sat in a bath full of
worms for four hours and fifty-
five minutes. We dug through
Grandad's gigantic steaming compost
heap and pulled out every worm we could find. It
took us all morning. Matt lost count after 9,183.

I didn't mind the worms wriggling around in my
ears, but I had to stop when some
of them started to crawl up my
nose. In fact, they were getting
everywhere. It definitely wasn't Ace.

Then we had to sneak all the worms out of the bath and back to the compost heap before Grandma realized what we were up to.

Is my four hours and fifty-five minutes in the worm bath a record?

Best wishes
Danny Baker

PS Grandad Nobby *is* the same person who broke the Blindfold One-foot Keepy-uppies Record. I've seen his certificate. It was signed by Alfred Bibby — is that your dad?
PPS While I sat in the bath of worms, Matthew tried to do Blindfold Keepy-uppies. He's only got up to three so far. It's really hard!

The Great Big Book
of World Records
London

ARE YOU A RECORD
BREAKER ?

Dear Danny

Thanks for letting me know about your brave
attempt on the Worm-bath Endurance record. You
were exactly seventy-three hours short. The
record is held by Wolfgang Walnuss of Germany.
He owned a worm farm in the town of Worms, and
gave every single worm a name. His favourite
was called Heidi.

Simply sitting in a bath of worms wasn't
enough for Wolfgang. He had a lifelong
ambition to *swim* in worms in Worms.

On the 15 June 1993, Wolfgang filled a swimming
pool with worms and plunged in, but after only
half a length, he sank to the bottom of the worm
pool. Everyone watching searched desperately in

the wriggling, writhing mass, but sadly Wolfgang
Walnuss drowned in worms in Worms.

However, he *did* set a new Worm-swimming world
record of 11.5 m, and his certificate is now
on display in the Worms Town Museum. No one
has ever tried to beat it. As Wolfgang's life
and death show, one worm may be wonderfully
wiggly, but dozens can be dangerously deadly.

Best wishes
Eric Bibby
Keeper of the Records

PS Alfred Bibby *was* my father. He became
fascinated with record-breaking quite by
chance one morning in 1951, when he discovered
the world's biggest ever earwig (34.4 cm long)
hiding in his left wellington boot. I have a
photo of him somewhere holding up the whopper!
If I can find it, I'll send you a copy.

That afternoon, the boys hurried across the farmyard with another bowl of Grandma's baked beans to add to the Pongy Potion.

'Don't you think we've put enough of those beans in?' asked Matthew.

'You can never have too many beans, Matt,' replied Danny. 'And if we don't put them in the potion, we'll have to *eat* them.'

Just then they heard a clanking sound coming from behind the pigsty. When they looked, the lid of the bucket was jumping up and down, as though something inside was trying to get out. Two long, greeny-yellow tentacles crept down the side of the bucket.

'The Pong's alive!' yelled Danny.

With a bang, the lid shot a metre into the air and clattered on to the ground at the boys' feet.

'It's escaping!' cried Matthew.

Danny held his nose, raced to the bucket, and threw in the beans. 'Come on, Matt, it's time to chuck the Pong Monster into Grandad's cowpat barrel before it gets away.'

They grabbed the bucket, and raced across the garden to the vegetable patch. The big wooden barrel stood just inside the gate.

Matthew shoved the lid to one side, and Danny tipped the steaming, bubbling, seething mixture into the thick, browny-black slop. The Pongy Potion floated on the surface for a moment before the cowpat sludge sucked it down hungrily.

LIQUID COWPATS

Suddenly, huge bubbles began to appear, bursting with loud, sloppy pops. The barrel started to grumble loudly.

'That sounds like Dad's stomach after he's had a chicken vindaloo,' laughed Danny.

Something knocked on the inside of the wooden tub. Long ropes of sticky slime spat into the air. The grumbling turned to rumbling and the top of the liquid started to bulge upwards.

'It's going to blow!' yelled Danny. 'It *is* like Dad's stomach after a chicken vindaloo! Run!'

The two boys charged towards the farmhouse as the cowpat barrel erupted with a ground-shaking 'BOOOOOMMM!'.

Danny glanced over his shoulder and saw a plume of browny-greeny-yellowy-black goo rocket into the air. As it climbed higher, it spread out like a fan, casting its smelly contents far and wide, and blotting out the sun.

The shadow of the approaching muck-cloud fell over Danny and Matthew. They nearly made it to the kitchen door, but not quite. They were just a few metres short when the Pong landed.

SPLAT!

The whole garden turned browny-greeny-yellowy-black.

Both boys had been turned into gooey gobs of greasy gloop.

'Ace!' said Danny, pulling a slimy old tea bag off

his head.

'Cool!'
agreed
Matthew.

Grandma
opened the
kitchen door.

'Oh, my days!' she cried. 'What's happened?'

'Grandad's cowpat barrel blew up!' answered
Danny.

'And we *stink*,' grinned Matthew.

'Not for long,' replied Grandma. 'Don't move!'

She marched off around the side of the house,
returning with the hosepipe.

'Keep still,' she ordered, and blasted the yucky
slime off the boys.

Grandad Nobby appeared at the door. 'How did
that get up there?' he asked, pointing to the sock
that dangled drippily from the TV aerial on the
roof.

Danny and Matthew glanced at each other.

'Cats?' suggested Danny.

'Bats?' suggested Matthew.

Grandad took off his old flat cap and scratched his head. He looked around at the mess that covered everything in sight. 'We'll have to hope it rains,' he said.

'Well then, we'd better do the Puddlethorpe Rain Dance,' said Grandma, and she and Grandad set off round the garden, jigging and wailing tunelessly. Danny and Matthew joined in, splashing in the shallow pools of dark sludge.

That evening it rained torrents. 'Never fails,' smiled Grandad, winking at the boys. 'This rain'll wash all that goo down into the ground. It'll be good for the soil, so no harm done.'

'There's harm done to my nose,' complained Grandma. 'What a whiff!'

Big

Danny woke early the next morning, got out of bed and opened the bedroom curtains.

He gasped.

He rubbed his eyes and looked again.

He gasped for a second time.

'Grandad! Grandma! Matt! Get up! Come and look at this!'

Danny raced downstairs and into the kitchen. He flung open the kitchen door and stared outside. He couldn't help it: he gasped once more.

The grass in the garden was two metres high. Buttercups, daisies and dandelions, with flowers as big as dinner-plates, stretched up above the tall green blades. Rose-bushes stood like small trees down one side of the garden, their branches bending under the weight of enormous white blooms. Other gigantic plants crushed and crowded together nearby, with towering spikes of red and blue flowers, huge purple bells and rafts of pink blossom.

Grandad, Grandma and Matthew joined Danny at the door.

'Oh, my giddy aunt!' exclaimed Grandma. 'I'm going to need a vase as big as a milk churn for those roses.'

'What about your vegetables, Mr B?' asked Matthew.

'My marrows!' yelled Grandad. 'Come on, let's go and see.'

They all pulled on their wellington boots and set off like jungle explorers, pushing aside the tall leaves, treading cautiously through the high grass that rustled noisily in the breeze.

Danny glimpsed woodlice as large as saucers, and spiders bigger than Grandad's hand, scurrying away into the shade.

All around them, but out of sight, hundreds of huge insects hummed and buzzed and clicked. Grandma moved an enormous buttercup leaf to one side, revealing a frog the size of a football staring back at them.

Danny laughed. 'Look at those big bulgy eyes – it looks like our teacher, Mrs Woodcock!'

'Yeah,' agreed Matthew. 'And she's got frog's legs too!'

As they emerged from the grass and gazed over the wall of the vegetable patch, Grandad jumped in the air like he'd scored a goal.

'My Rotting Chowhabunga!' he cried, pointing at his treasured plant.

It was normally a small spiky clump of bright green waxy leaves. Now it was almost as tall as the boys, and rising from the centre was a thick stalk with a large dark flower-bud on the end.

'It's going to flower!' said Grandad. 'For the first time *ever* in a pot! It's a miracle!'

Danny grinned at Matthew and winked.

'And my marrows are massive!' exclaimed Grandad. 'My carrots are colossal! My lettuces are leviathans! My gooseberries are gargantuan! My parsnips are . . .' He thought for a moment '. . . pretty big!'

Grandad's grin got wider.

'If Ernie Slack can beat these beauties, I'll eat my cap!' He rubbed his hands together. 'We'll pick the best tomorrow morning and enter them for the competition at the Fair. *This* year, victory will be mine!'

A Spot of Bother in the Vegetable Patch

The Great Big Book
of World Records
London

Dear Danny

Here's the photo I promised you of the
humongous earwig! This creature inspired my
father to track down and measure the biggest
bugs from all over the world, and he donated
many of his specimens to Creepy-Crawly
Creek, a Wildlife Park and Home for Rescued
Invertebrates at Bugsby Tyke. It's actually

Dad, 1951

not far from Puddlethorpe, and I think *you* would love it, because it's a record-breaking kind of place!

They have ants as thick as your thumb, centipedes as long as your leg and slugs as fat as your fist. They have a Spider City, a Beetle Boulevard and a Cockroach Corner. They also have Gastropod Grove, which contains the largest collection of slugs and snails in the world, all slithering and sliming around in a massive compound. This is officially the Slimiest Place in the World, and *has* to be worth a visit!

Best wishes
Eric Bibby
Keeper of the Records

PS The little boy with knobbly knees standing next to my father is me! Believe it or not, I do not have the Knobbliest Knees in the world. That record is held by Alfie Smee, of Beaumont-cum-Moze, whose horrible, ugly knees could make grown women faint and small children cry. They were *so* bad that on 13 May 1932 a Special Law was passed banning Alfie Smee's knees from ever being shown in public.

It was the morning of the Puddlethorpe
Annual Country Fair. Danny and
Matthew sat at the kitchen
table, flicking through a
book called *What's That
Bug?*. Nine enormous pickle
jars, their lids punched
with air holes, were lined up
in front of them, each one
containing a huge crawling insect.

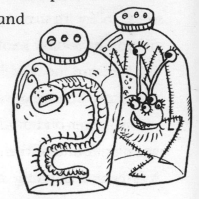

Grandma studied the specimens with interest.

'My,' she said, 'you two *have* been busy. What are
you going to do with these beasties?'

'We're trying to find out what they're called,'
answered Danny. 'Matt's going to measure them
all and I'm going to write to Mr Bibby at *The Great
Big Book of World Records* to see if any of them are
world-beaters.'

Matthew grinned at Danny. 'Imagine if your
sister Natalie found a couple of these under her
duvet . . . !'

Grandad put his head round the kitchen door.

'Hurry up, you two,' he said. 'I'm going to need some help with my vegetables. The sooner they're picked, the sooner we can get to the Fair.'

'OK, Grandad. We'll finish doing this later.' The boys pulled on their wellies and went outside.

The flower-bud on the Rotting Chowhabunga was bigger and darker.

'I think today's the day,' said Grandad excitedly.

'Will the flower *really* stink?' asked Matthew, eyeing the plant warily.

'So I've been told, but I don't know for sure. I've never smelt one.'

Grandad led the way along the narrow path they had cleared through the jungle the day before, towards the gate. The grass, buttercups and dandelions waved high above them in the breeze. As he stepped out, the boys heard him cry out in dismay.

'Oh no! My prize-winners!'

Danny and Matthew ran to his side and looked over the wall. What they saw made their jaws drop.

The vegetable patch was a seething, writhing

mass of gigantic pink worms each at least four
metres long and as thick as a goalpost.
They looked more like pythons
than worms, as they crawled,
slithered and slid over the
huge plants, sucking and
slurping great holes out of
them.

'Gross!' said Danny.

'Double-gross!' added Matthew.

'Quick!' shouted Grandad, grabbing a
wheelbarrow. 'We've got to get the good vegetables
out before those beasts eat them all!'

He trundled his barrow through the gate towards
the one remaining untouched marrow. The boys
helped him lift it into the barrow, then Danny raced
towards the runner beans, while Matthew grabbed
a spade and headed for the onions.

'Only pick the good ones!' called Grandad,
thwacking a monster worm with his flat cap.

Danny had collected an armful of enormous
runner beans when he felt the earth shudder and

shift under his feet. The head of a giant earthworm
burst out of the soil, stretching and quivering
towards the beans.

Three worms emerged from the ground nearby
and headed for the sprouts. Two more appeared by
the peas, while others popped up at various places
around the patch and began to creep towards

the middle, all heading for

Grandad's marrow.

Grandma Florrie ran up

to the gate.

'Lawks-a-lordy!' she

howled. 'What are we going

to do?'

'Call Creepy-crawly Creek in

Bugsby Tyke!'

Danny

shouted.

'Tell them we're

surrounded.

They'll know

what to do!'

The Worm Wranglers of Creepy-crawly Creek

Danny scanned the vegetable patch. In a far corner by the gate he spied a large stack of sun-dried cowpats that were piled up ready to be taken to the Fair for the cowpat-hurling contest.

'Come on, Matt, let's get 'em!'

Danny and Matthew began to skim the hard, flat pooh-projectiles at the wiggling monster worms as they burst from their burrows and lunged at the vegetables. Grandad stood guard by his precious marrow, fending off incoming attackers with his spade and cap.

Despite their efforts, the huge worms kept coming. Just when the boys' cowpat ammunition supply was starting to run low, a bright red truck skidded to a halt on the other side of the wall, six yellow lights on top of the cab flashing urgently. Emblazoned along the side of the vehicle were the words:

CREEPY-CRAWLY
CREEK
EMERGENCY WORM-WRANGLING TEAM
'We're Bugsby Tyke's finest!'
(NO JOB TOO LARGE OR TOO WRIGGLY)

A woman and two men jumped down from the truck. They wore lime-green, wipe-clean, slime-proof zip-tight boiler suits, and carried large yellow buckets in their red-rubber-gloved hands.

Hammers, pincers and lassos dangled from their shiny black belts.

'I'm Babs, Chief Worm Wrangler,' announced the woman as she rushed through the gate. 'And this is my team, Bernie and Butch.'

She saw the giant worms slithering all over the vegetable patch. 'Whoa! This is *serious*!'

'We're going to need bigger buckets!' yelled Bernie.

'We're going to need wheelie bins!' barked Butch.

Babs surveyed the scene. 'Right! Here's the plan!' She pointed at Danny and Matthew. 'You lads keep pelting these monsters with cowpats.'

She pointed at Grandma. 'Mrs Baker, take Butch to the wheelie bins.'

She turned to the third Worm Wrangler.

'Bernie, call Base Control. Tell them to get High Containment Unit X1-2000 ready. These are Super Worms we're dealing with!'

When Butch returned with the wheelie bins, Babs slapped Danny and Matthew on the back. 'Well done, lads,' she said. 'You've done a great job. Now it's time to let the professionals take over.'

Babs and Bernie unhooked their lassos and took up position by the marrow in the barrow, snagging each mammoth worm that appeared above ground. As the ropes tightened, the struggling creatures were dragged out of their burrows, and flung wriggling and writhing into the bins. Butch slammed the lids shut as the worms battered against them, trying to escape.

At last the vegetable patch was clear. Babs turned to Grandad. 'The situation's under control now, Mr Baker. You can pick your vegetables and get off to the Fair.'

She strode over to the boys. 'Thanks for all your help, lads. I've never seen worms this big in Yorkshire! The wheelie bins won't hold them for long – we need to get them into the High Containment Unit X1-2000 asap.'

Babs reached into a pocket of her lime-green, wipe-clean, slime-proof zip-tight boiler suit. 'Here's four free tickets for Creepy-crawly Creek,' she said, handing them to Danny. 'You can come and see your worms any time.'

She jumped into the truck next to Bernie and Butch, winked at the boys and, with lights flashing, sped off towards Bugsby Tyke.

'Come on!' said Grandad, grabbing his vegetables. 'Let's get going. I can't wait to see Ernie Slack's face when he catches sight of this little lot!'

Ernie Slack

As usual, Grandad's neighbour Tom Abson
had made room in his Low Meadow for the
Puddlethorpe Annual County Fair. The field was
a hotch potch of animal pens, stalls and sideshow
attractions, and at its centre stood the candy-striped
canopy of the main marquee, surrounded by a
makeshift racetrack.

Danny and Matthew helped Grandad Nobby
carry his enormous vegetables into the marquee,
where the judging would take place later. Tables
ran around the edge, all covered in clean, crisp
white cloths. They were
crammed with vegetables
of all shapes and sizes,
arranged either neatly
in little piles, or
as large, single
specimens. The
table carrying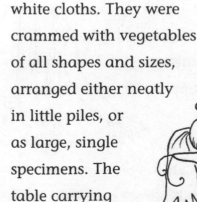

Grandad's massive marrow, beautiful beans and cracking carrots bowed in the middle with their weight.

Grandad placed a small card with his name on in front of them. He beamed with pleasure.

'You're going to win for sure, Grandad,' said Danny.

At that moment Ernie Slack strode towards them, dragging with him the Chief Judge, Mr Willis. Ernie was as long, thin and stringy as one of Grandad's runner beans, and his long, thin, stringy black moustache curled at each end like a pig's tail.

'You must disqualify Nobby Baker this instant!' he demanded. 'Those vegetables aren't normal – he's cheating!'

Judge Willis raised an eyebrow. 'They're certainly extraordinary, Ernie. But I can't see any reason to disqualify Nobby.'

Ernie blustered and fumed, and the ends of his curly moustache twitched with temper, but Danny could see that he knew Judge Willis was right. Ernie Slack stomped away.

Grandad grinned and turned to the boys. 'The judging's this afternoon, right after the Puddlethorpe Grand National,' he said. He handed them five pounds each. 'You lads go and enjoy yourselves.'

Danny and Matthew thanked Grandad and went out into the bright late-summer sunshine. The hubbub of the crowd mixed with the bleating of sheep and the lowing of cows. The boys bought a hot dog each, listened to the Puddlethorpe Cowbell Ringers, and then tried out the fun and games. Danny managed to Dunk the Vicar, and won a pen shaped like a turnip. Matthew had had so much practice zapping worms that morning that he easily took first prize in the Junior Cowpat-Hurling Competition, and won a gold medallion in the shape of a cowpat.

'Ace!' said Danny.

'Cool!' agreed Matthew as they compared prizes.

Soon, everyone at the Fair began to gather for the main event of the afternoon: the Puddlethorpe Grand National. Six pantomime horses, each made up of two people and carrying a scarecrow jockey, lined up to race around a course that circled the main marquee. Danny spotted Grandma and Grandad in the crowd, and the boys pushed through to join them.

Tom Abson's voice boomed out over a loudspeaker in the centre of the field. 'Welcome to the thirty-eighth year of our famous race. The runners and riders are ready. Keep your eye on last year's winner, Ee By Gum, in the pink.'

The crowd began to cheer, calling out the names of their favourite horses. The referee held his starting pistol in the air and with a loud *CRACK!* the race began.

'And they're off!' yelled Tom Abson. 'There's a lot of bumping and banging going on as they

jockey for position coming up to the first hurdle . . .
Whoops-a-daisy . . .'

Three horses tumbled at the fence, where they
lay struggling and tangled up on the grass. Ee By
Gum and Ecky Thump went over safely.

The commentary continued. 'Coming up to the
next hurdle, and Ee By Gum's over, Ecky Thump's
over . . . Oh no! What a Load of Baloney is down
and he's lost his head! Don't look children, it's
horrible!'

Ee By Gum and Ecky Thump raced neck and neck
around the rest of the course. It was still close going
over the final hurdle, but then Ee By Gum jumped
two feet in the air and began to twitch and kick.

'There's something
wrong inside Ee By Gum,'
declared Tom Abson. 'If
I'm not mistaken, it
looks like they've got a
bee on board.'

Suddenly, Ee By Gum
went off course, charged into

Ecky Thump and bowled over several spectators. The pantomime horse bucked and pranced across the winning line as the two men inside were stung by the bee.

The crowd cheered and clapped. People at the back craned their necks to get a better look. Danny turned to say something to Matthew, and the smile dropped from his face. Over his friend's shoulder, Danny saw Ernie Slack sneaking into the empty marquee, wielding a huge axe.

'Grandad!' he yelled.

'Stop him!' shouted Grandad, but no one heard his voice above the noise of the crowd roaring at the pantomime horses. The boys began to force their way through the press of people behind them, to get to the marquee.

'It's no good,' said Danny. 'We'll never get there in time!'

Stinky

The loudspeakers set around the field let out a loud wet coughing sound that silenced the crowd.

'What's that awful pong?' spluttered Tom Abson. 'It's like boiled cabbage and seaweed and eggs and cheese and drains all mixed together.'

'My Rotting Chowhabunga!' cried Grandad. 'The flower must have opened!'

The animals in pens near the marquee became agitated.

The sheep went 'Moo'.

The cows went 'Baa'.

The geese went 'Woof'.

The pigs didn't seem bothered at all.

People fled, holding their noses in disgust. The stink was truly terrible.

Danny spied a hardware stall nearby, and grabbed a handful of wooden pegs.

'This worked when I had toxic toes,' he explained. He clipped one on to his nose, and handed out the others.

Pegs in place, Grandad, Grandma and the boys hurried into the marquee. A shocking sight met their eyes: Ernie Slack stood over Grandad's marrow, the axe raised high above his head, ready to strike.

'No!' yelled Grandad. 'Stop!'

But Ernie Slack *had* stopped. He was as stiff as a statue.

The big pot containing the Rotting Chowhabunga plant stood on a table in the centre of the marquee. The thick, purple star-shaped flower was open, and looked like a hand reaching up to the sky.

'The story was true!' said Grandad.

'Ace!' cried Danny.

'Cool!' agreed Matthew.

The boys ran forward. 'Has he *really* been turned into stone?' Matthew wondered.

Danny prodded Ernie Slack's tummy and it wobbled a little. 'No,' he replied, disappointed. 'He's just sort of . . . frozen.'

'You'd better take some photos of your flower before it dies,' suggested Grandma.

'Aye, I will,' replied Grandad. 'But first I'm going to get evidence.' He pulled a camera out of his pocket, and took photographs of Ernie Slack about to do his dastardly deed.

'Boys, go and find Judge Willis,' said Grandma. 'Tell him to put a peg on his nose and come quick. He needs to see this.'

Danny and Matthew returned with Judge Willis, and while the grown-ups tutted and shook their heads at the frozen cheat, the boys picked up the pot containing the Rotting Chowhabunga and heaved it out of the big tent. They carried it to the far end of the field, and placed it under an old pear tree.

'It shouldn't do any harm over here,' said Danny.

Immediately four calling birds, three French hens, two turtle doves and a partridge plummeted senseless from the branches of the pear tree on to the grass below.

'This *must* be the stinkiest flower in the world,' said Danny.

'It's awesome,' admired Matthew. 'Not as bad as your feet though.'

'No,' agreed Danny. 'Not *that* bad.'

When they got back to the main marquee, the paralysing effect of the Rotting Chowhabunga's stink had worn off, and Ernie Slack had thawed out. He stood like a naughty schoolboy before Judge Willis and the huge crowd of spectators.

'Because of your unsportsmanlike behaviour, you are disqualified from this year's competition,' the judge said sternly. He reached into the top pocket of his jacket and brandished a red card.

Ernie's face darkened, like a little thunder cloud about to burst, and his curly black moustache nearly twitched off his face. The crowd booed and hissed as he slunk from the marquee.

Judge Willis held up his hand and everyone fell silent. 'Ladies and gentlemen, let the judging begin!'

It was an agonizing wait, as the judges judged. One by one, they pronounced the winners of the Spottiest Cow, the Pig with the Curliest Tail, the Sheep with the Loudest Baa, the Sweetest Rose, the Sunniest Marigold, the Crustiest Loaf, the Most Tear-jerking Onion . . .

At last Judge Willis declared, 'The winner of First Prize for Most Massive Marrow in Show goes to . . . Nobby Baker!'

'Yessssssssssssssssssss!' cried Grandad, Grandma, Danny and Matthew together.

Grandad also won Blue Rosettes for the Longest Carrot and Stringiest Beans. Finally Judge Willis announced, 'We have one extra-special award to give, one that we have never awarded before and I hope will never *ever* award again. The prize for the Stinkiest Flower in Show goes to Nobby Baker!'

Everyone clapped and cheered. Grandad beamed with joy.

When the award ceremony was over, the judges came to shake hands with Grandad.

'So, Nobby, what's the special ingredient you've been feeding your vegetables with this year?' asked Judge Willis. Grandad tapped the side of his nose with his finger. 'It's a secret.' He smiled.

'A *super* secret!' exclaimed Danny and Matthew.

'I just wish I knew what the super secret was,' admitted Grandad when the judge had gone.

Nobby Baker -
Record Breaker

Crag Top Farm
Puddlethorpe

Dear Mr Bibby

For once I'm not asking about a
record for me, I'm writing about
my grandad, Nobby. Yesterday at the
Puddlethorpe Annual Country Fair his
Rotting Chowhabunga plant finally flowered for
the very first time. It was the stinkiest flower
I've ever smelt.

Grandad

Grandad says that this is
the first time a Rotting
Chowhabunga has ever
flowered in captivity. Is this

TOXIC!

Phewee

true, and does that make my grandad a record breaker?

Best wishes
Danny Baker

PS I've sent a picture of the flower to prove he did it. It's lucky for you I didn't take it with a Smello-vision camera!

Totally stinky →

ARE YOU A RECORD
BREAKER ?

Dear Danny,

Thank you for your letter. Actually, I *have*
smelt the Rotting Chowhabunga flower. I once
went to the Amazon jungle just to smell it. The
local people know when the flower is about to
open, because the forest clears of animals just
before it happens. Flocks of birds rise from the
trees and troupes of monkeys flee in panic. The
smell reminded me of boiled cabbage and seaweed
and eggs and cheese and drains all mixed
together. Because of the legend, I was careful
not to get too close, but even at a distance of
fifteen metres my nose went numb and my toes
began to tingle! I'm very glad I wasn't in that
marquee at the Fair when the flower opened.

I have checked all my records and it's true:

this is the first time the Rotting Chowhabunga
has been made to flower outside the jungles
of Brazil. Your grandad *is* a record breaker,
and it gives me great pleasure to enclose his
certificate.

Best wishes,
Eric Bibby
Keeper of the Records

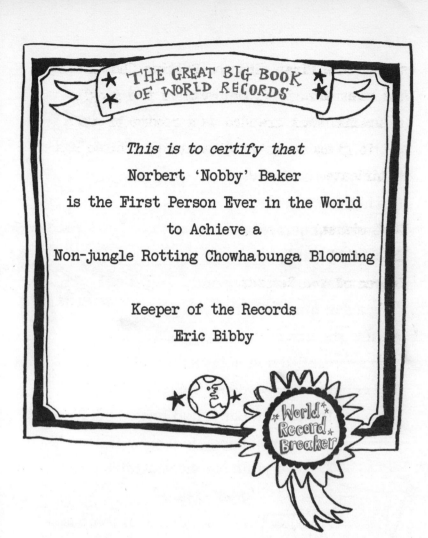

THE GREAT BIG BOOK
OF WORLD RECORDS

This is to certify that
Norbert 'Nobby' Baker
is the First Person Ever in the World
to Achieve a
Non-jungle Rotting Chowhabunga Blooming

Keeper of the Records
Eric Bibby

World Record Breaker

'Do you mind me getting one of these instead of you, Danny?' asked Grandad.

'No, 'course not,' replied Danny. 'We had loads of fun helping you win it.'

Grandma glanced up from the little pink baby bonnet she was knitting, and frowned at him. 'What do you mean?' she asked.

Danny smiled a naughty smile, and explained how adding the Pongy Potion to the cowpat barrel had caused the Rotting Chowhabunga to flower, and made everything in the vegetable patch grow so huge.

'And the great thing is, you can beat Ernie Slack *every* year!' said Danny.

Matthew held up a piece of paper. 'Because I wrote down

the Pongy Potion recipe!'

Grandma put down her knitting and looked at the list Matthew had made. 'You used my home-made baked beans!' she complained.

Danny tapped the side of his nose. '*They* must have been the Super-Secret Ingredient!' he said.

A NOTE FROM THE AUTHOR

DANNY BAKER RECORD BREAKER

Dear Mr Bibby

I've got a new website! Ace! Now I can tell people what I'm up to, and other kids can tell me about their record attempts. If they're really mega I'll send them certificates and stickers. There's loads of great stuff on the site, like:

- Gross recipes
- The world's stinkiest records
- Awesome activities
- Videos of people breaking records
- Competitions, und loads more!

Could this be the Wackiest Website Ever?

Best wishes

Danny Baker

DANNY BAKER RECORD BREAKER

THE WORLD'S BIGGEST BOGEY

STEVE HARTLEY

TO THE MANAGER
The Great Big Book
of World Records
London

Dear Sir,
I have been collecting bogeys
from my nose for the last two years.
I have stuck them all together to make
one enormous bogey. It measures
5·3 cm in diameter and weighs
3·6 grams. Is this a record?

Yours faithfully,

Danny Baker

(Aged nine and a bit)

WARNING! THIS STORY MAY CONTAIN SILLINESS

Join Danny as he attempts to smash a
load of revolting records, including:

FREE STICKERS

LOUDEST TRUMP!
CHEESIEST FEET!
NITTIEST SCALP!

OUT NOW!

DANNY BAKER RECORD BREAKER

LOOK OUT FOR TWO NEW DANNY
BAKER BOOKS, COMING IN JULY 2010!

THE WORLD'S LOUDEST ARMPIT FART

and

THE WORLD'S STICKIEST EARWAX

WARNING! GROSSEST RECORDS YET!

A selected list of titles available from Macmillan Children's Books

The prices shown below are correct at the time of going to press. However, Macmillan Publishers reserves the right to show new retail prices on covers, which may differ from those previously advertised.

Steve Hartley
Danny Baker Record Breaker:
   The World's Biggest Bogey   978-0-330-50916-9   £4.99

Andy Griffiths & Terry Denton
Help! My Parents Think I'm a Robot
   (and 9 other Just Shocking! stories)   978-0-330-45426-1   £4.99
Help! I'm Being Chased by a Giant Slug
   (and 8 other Just Disgusting! stories)   978-0-330-50411-9   £4.99
What Bumosaur Is That?   978-0-330-44752-2   £4.99

Paul Stewart & Chris Riddell
Blobheads   978-0-330-41353-8   £4.99
Blobheads Go Boing!   978-0-330-43181-1   £4.99

All Pan Macmillan titles can be ordered from our website, www.panmacmillan.com, or from your local bookshop and are also available by post from:

Bookpost, PO Box 29, Douglas, Isle of Man IM99 1BQ

Credit cards accepted. For details:
Telephone: 01624 677237
Fax: 01624 670923
Email: bookshop@enterprise.net
www.bookpost.co.uk

Free postage and packing in the United Kingdom